Magic
Animal Friends

Special thanks to Valerie Wilding

ORCHARD BOOKS
Carmelite House
50 Victoria Embankment
London EC4Y 0DZ

A Paperback Original

First published in 2015 by Orchard Books

Text © Working Partners Ltd 2015
Illustrations © Orchard Books 2015

A CIP catalogue record for this book is available
from the British Library.

ISBN 978 1 40833 881 0

1 3 5 7 9 8 6 4 2

MIX
Paper from
responsible sources
FSC® C104740
www.fsc.org

The paper and board used in this book are made from wood
from responsible sources.

Orchard Books
An imprint of Hachette Children's Group
Part of The Watts Publishing Group Limited
An Hachette UK Company

Evie Scruffypup's Big Surprise

Daisy Meadows

ORCHARD

Honey
Tree

Sunshine
Meadow

Mr Cleverfeather's
Inventing Shed

Goldie's Grotto

Toadstool
Cafe

Toadstool Glade

Parasol
Tree

Mrs Taptree's
Library

Grizelda's
Workshop

Friendship
Tree

Sparr
Fall

Rushing Rapids

Entrance
to the Caverns

Butterfly
Bowery

Nibblesqueak Bakery

Map of Friendship Forest

Woollyhop Shop

Harmony Hall Theatre

Petal Hill

Garland Green

Cherry Tree Corner

Treasure Tree

Bluebell Brook

Agatha Glitterwing's Shop

Slipperslide's Home

Sparklepaw Cottage

Coral Cove

Summer Sands Beach

Grizelda's Tower

Witchy Waste

Can you keep a secret? I thought you could!

Then I'll tell you about an enchanted wood.

It lies through the door in the old oak tree,

Let's go there now - just follow me!

We'll find adventure that never ends,

And meet the Magic Animal Friends!

Love

Goldie the Cat

Contents

CHAPTER ONE

An Autumn Visitor

Jess Forester shuffled her foot through a pile of crisp, fallen leaves. "There are loads of chestnuts here!" she said. She and her best friend, Lily Hart, were in Jess's garden, filling a box with fallen nuts.

"They'll be a treat for the squirrel my mum and dad are looking after," said Lily.

The squirrel was one of the patients at Helping Paw Wildlife Hospital, which was across the road from Jess's house. Lily's parents ran it, and the two girls loved animals so much that they helped out whenever they could.

A flurry of deep gold leaves drifted down from the tree.

Jess caught one. "I love autumn colours, don't you?" she said. "There's yellow and red and— look!" She pointed up through the branches. "There! A squirrel!" she said.

More leaves tumbled down as the squirrel bounded higher.

"He's so sweet!" said Lily. "Maybe he'll come to us if I offer him a chestnut."

She held one out, but the squirrel stayed on the branch, watching them nervously.

"He's shy. Let's leave some here for him," Jess suggested, heaping a handful of nuts on the grass.

"I wish we could tell him it's safe to come down," said Lily. "After all, we've spoken to squirrels before, in Friendship Forest!"

Jess grinned. Friendship Forest was a secret world where the animals lived in little cottages and visited the Toadstool Café and, best of all – they talked! One of them, a cat called Goldie, was the girls' special friend. She had taken them on lots of exciting adventures in the forest.

"I wish Goldie would visit us soon," Lily sighed.

Jess nudged her, pointing to a nearby tree. "She's here now!" she said in delight.

A pair of green eyes, the colour of grass in the evening sun, blinked from between the yellow leaves.

"Goldie!" the girls cried.

A beautiful golden cat leaped from the tree and ran to press against their legs, purring.

The girls bent to stroke her.

"Does this mean Friendship Forest needs our help?" wondered Lily. "Is Grizelda causing trouble for the animals?"

 13

Grizelda was a wicked witch. So far Jess, Lily and Goldie had managed to stop her plans to take over the forest, but now Grizelda had four helpers – messy creatures from the Witchy Waste.

The Witchy Waste had once been a beautiful water garden, with willow trees, ponds and waterlilies. Then Grizelda's creatures had made it as filthy as a rubbish tip. Now she wanted them to help her make Friendship Forest messy and horrible too, so all the animals would have to leave.

The last time Jess and Lily were in

14

Friendship Forest, Peep the bat from the Witchy Waste put a spell on Olivia Nibblesqueak, a sweet little hamster. The spell made Olivia as messy as Peep, and had started to turn her into a cheeky bat, too! The girls had managed to undo Peep's spell, but they knew that three more Witchy Waste creatures were waiting to cause trouble.

Goldie mewed as she turned towards the gate.

"Come on, Lily!" Jess hopped with excitement. "Goldie's taking us to Friendship Forest!"

The girls ran down the lane, hurrying past the wildlife hospital. Two baby rabbits sat up inside their run, looking startled as they dashed by.

Goldie led them over the stepping stones in the stream at the bottom of Lily's garden, and into Brightley Meadow. In the middle stood an old oak tree with bare, lifeless branches.

The Friendship Tree!

Jess and Lily shared an excited glance as Goldie reached the tree. Something amazing was about to happen!

Sure enough, leaves sprang from every

16

branch — but they weren't the bright spring green they usually were. This time, the leaves unfurled in glorious autumn colours — red, yellow, orange and gold. They glowed in the sunshine. Bluebirds and robins swooped down to feast on the scarlet berries that hung from every twig.

Goldie stretched up a paw and patted some words carved into the tree trunk. Jess and Lily read the words aloud: "Friendship Forest!"

A door with a leaf-shaped handle appeared in the trunk. Jess opened it, and a soft golden light gleamed from inside.

17

Goldie slipped through the door.

The girls held hands excitedly as they
followed her into the shimmering glow.

A tingle ran right through them. Jess
and Lily knew that meant they were
shrinking, just a little.

As the light faded, they found themselves in a clearing in Friendship Forest. It was always summer in the forest, and today the warm air was sweet with the popcorn scent of nearby butterpuff bushes. Little cottages were tucked among the shady tree roots.

"It's wonderful to be back," Jess began, then gasped in surprise.

Every tree was covered in a glorious blanket of blossom.

"Wow! There are so many colours," said Lily, gazing up in wonder.

"Isn't it beautiful?" said a soft voice.

The girls spun round. Their cat friend was standing upright, wearing her glittering golden scarf!

"Goldie! At last we can talk to you!" cried Lily as she ran to hug her.

"It's a very special time in Friendship Forest," said Goldie, smiling. "Today is Blossom Day!"

CHAPTER TWO

Blossom Day

"What's Blossom Day?" Lily asked.

"Once every year," Goldie explained, "all the trees bloom. Doesn't it look gorgeous?"

"It smells gorgeous, too!" said Jess. "Like honey and plums and jasmine and cherryade all mixed together!"

 21

"It's even better at Petal Hill," Goldie replied. "That's where we celebrate Blossom Day. Come with me!"

On the way, Jess and Lily gazed up at the dazzling petals that covered the trees.

"Those ones are so pretty!" Jess said in wonder, pointing out a cluster of purple blossoms that looked like fluffy pompoms.

Lily spotted some white flowers trailing down from the branches. "Look, they're like beautiful strings of pearls!" she said.

Soon they reached a round hill, dotted with blossom-covered shrubs.

At the foot of the hill was a rambling

den with blue walls and a steep red roof. Yellow and white striped curtains billowed at the open windows. All around it was a garden, filled with colourful flower beds, tall trees – and lots of their animal friends!

"Hello, everyone!" called Lily and Jess.

There were squeaks, quacks and squawks of delight from the young animals.

Bella Tabbypaw the kitten hugged them, purring loudly. Molly Twinkletail the mouse and her nine brothers and sisters called ten greetings. Lola Velvetnose

 23

the mole hugged Lily's leg.

"Girls!" said Goldie.

Jess and Lily turned to see Goldie standing with a family of dogs with thick tufty black and white fur, pointed ears and madly wagging tails.

"Meet Mr and Mrs Scruffypup," said Goldie, "and their daughters, Evie and Hattie."

The excited pups hugged the girls.

"Hello!" said Hattie. She was as tall as the girls' waists, and had a blue bow on her head.

"Hello, Lily! Hello, Jess!" said Evie and

hugged both of them, her tail wagging. She had dark, sparkling eyes, and was wearing pink glasses. She was smaller than her sister and her fur was far scruffier, sticking up in little tufts.

Mr Scruffypup laughed as the pups jumped down. "We're glad to meet you, Jess and Lily," he said. "We've heard about how brave you've been, standing up to Grizelda. Come in, come in! Everyone wants to see you!"

A tiny golden hamster ran towards them, and Jess scooped her up. "Hi, Olivia Nibblesqueak!" she said.

"I'm so glad you've come," the little hamster said.

"Me too," said Evie eagerly. "We're going to start the blossom drop hunt soon and you can join in!"

"That sounds fun," said Lily with a laugh, "but what is the blossom drop hunt?"

"We have it every Blossom Day," Mrs Scruffypup explained. "Blossom drops are special tasty treats – the Nibblesqueak family makes them in their bakery, from honeysuckle blossoms. Mr Scruffypup and I hide them all around Petal Hill and everyone tries to find as many as they can!"

Evie bounced up and down with excitement. "Can we start the hunt now, Mum? Please?"

"Please! We can't wait!" cried the other little animals, gathering around Mr and Mrs Scruffypup.

Mr Scruffpup chuckled. "We can't start quite yet," he said. "We need Mr Cleverfeather to get here first. I wonder where he could be?"

Jess gave a cry as she spotted an old owl, wearing a waistcoat and monocle, hurrying towards Petal Hill. Under one wing was tucked a machine that looked like a mini vacuum cleaner. "Here he comes!" she said.

"Lorry I'm sate," panted the owl as he reached them, muddling up his words like he always did. "I mean, sorry I'm late. I've got my Peffal Putter," he said, patting the machine, "so we can start the hunt!"

"He means Petal Puffer," Goldie whispered to the girls with a grin.

"Thank you, Mr Cleverfeather," said Mrs Scruffypup. "Now, when the petal puffer puffs, the hunt for the blossom drops begins!

Lily, Jess, Goldie and the little animals lined up excitedly in front of Mr Cleverfeather. Evie was holding onto her big sister's paw, her tail wagging with excitement.

"Petals ready! Puffer steady! Go!" Mr Cleverfeather hooted.

He pressed a button and the Puffer

whooshed thousands of petals high up above them. They drifted slowly downwards like colourful confetti. With squeals of delight, the animals ran off to hunt for blossom drops. Lola Velvetnose and Olivia Nibblequeak ran into the den, while Bella Tabbypaw darted over to search in a flowerbed.

"Look!" Bella cried, holding up a little parcel made of leaves. "I've found some blossom drops!"

"Let's search in the treehouse," said Hattie. "It's this way!"

The girls and Goldie ran after the two

puppies as they bounded over to a huge
old apple tree. Built all around the trunk,
and reaching up into the branches, was
the most amazing wooden treehouse
they'd ever seen.

"Wow!" gasped Jess as she stared up at
the different levels. There were curtains at
the windows and pretty flowers painted
all around the door.

"Dad made it," said Evie. "Me and Hattie have loads of fun in here. Let's see if there are any blossom drops inside!"

Evie and Hattie climbed into the tree house. Then they vanished from sight!

"Where are you?" Lily called up to them.

"Surprise!" Evie giggled, popping up at a third floor window.

"Hi!" cried Hattie, looking

out of a door on the second level.

Evie disappeared for a moment, then

leaned out of the topmost window. "Boo!"

Laughing, the girls and Goldie followed

them inside. More flowers were painted

on the walls, and they went up a wooden

ladder to the next level, where Evie and

Hattie were searching through a huge

pile of toys.

Evie give a *yip* of excitement, and

from inside a box of wooden animals she

pulled out a small packet made of leaves

tied with grass strands.

"Surprise!" Evie called. "Blossom drops!"

She handed the parcel to Lily, who opened it. Inside were lots of oval, honeysuckle-scented treats.

"Mmm!" Lily said as she ate one. "It's gooey in the middle! That was a surprise."

Evie giggled and Hattie pulled her into a hug. "Evie loves surprises!" Hattie said, ruffling her little sister's tufty fur.

They all jumped as there was a terrified squeal.

"Eeeeeeeek!"

It came from the Scruffypups' den.

 35

"What was that?" asked Goldie, her tail twitching with worry.

They hurried out of the treehouse. Little animals were bursting out of the front door of the den, scurrying to their parents. The girls and Goldie ran over. Through the windows, they could see a rat, a crow, a toad and a bat charging through the den, chasing the frightened animals.

"The creatures from the Witchy Waste!" cried Lily. "They're stealing all the blossom drops!"

CHAPTER THREE

Masha's Spell

"Come on!" cried Lily as she, Jess and Goldie ran into the den.

The Witchy Waste creatures were hurtling around the Scruffypups' kitchen. Snippit the crow flapped his tatty wings at Lola Velvetnose the mole. She'd dropped her big purple-framed glasses, and didn't

 37

see him until he was right next to her. She shrieked and knocked over some saucepans. "This way, Lola!" called Goldie, helping her to the door.

Masha the rat waved her straw hat as she pushed the kitchen chairs over. "Yee-ha!" she cried.

"This is fun!"

Lily scooped Olivia Nibblesqueak
out of the teacup she was hiding inside.
"You're safe now," she told the tiny
hamster, as she carried her outside and
placed her on the grass.

"Stop it! You're scaring everyone!" Jess
shouted.

Hopper the toad crawled out from
under the kitchen table. She poked her
wide, flat tongue out at Jess. Peep the
bat landed on a shelf,
giggling as he sent
a stack of plates

crashing to the floor. "Lovely mess!" he
squeaked.

There were frightened cries from
outside the den. Through the window,
the girls saw a familiar yellow-green orb
floating over Petal Hill.

"Oh no!" groaned Lily, as they ran
back out of the den.

Cra-ack! The orb burst into smelly
yellow-green sparks.

Mr Cleverfeather flapped backwards as
the sparks cleared, revealing Grizelda in
her purple tunic. Her skinny black trousers
were tucked into shiny boots with thin

high heels. The witch's green hair hung
around her shoulders like wet seaweed as
she threw back her head, cackling.

"It's the meddling girls and the
interfering cat," Grizelda said. "You might
have stopped Peep's fun, but Masha,
Snippit and Hopper haven't cast their
spells yet." Her dark eyes glittered as she
pointed at the watching animals with a
bony finger. "Soon Masha will use her
magic on one of you – then you'll turn
into a messy rat too!"

Jess, Lily and Goldie stood their ground
as the animals ran and hid, squealing.

Grizelda laughed. "The spell will make whoever it touches love messiness as much as Masha and her friends. Soon, the forest will be filled with creatures who love rubbish and dirt! Friendship Forest will become so filthy that all you silly animals will have to leave. Ha haa!"

Jess shouted bravely, "You won't win!"

"We'll see about that!" Grizelda

snapped her fingers and disappeared in a
burst of spitting sparks.

The animals were staring at each other
in horror. A flash of movement caught
Lily's eye – Masha the rat was scuttling
towards Evie!

"Look out!" Lily yelled.

But Masha had already reached the
little puppy. She turned around and shook
her long pink tail. A shower of purple
sparks cascaded over Evie.

Goldie's paws flew to her mouth. "Oh
no!" she cried.

Evie shook her tufty fur. She sat still

for a moment, but she looked exactly the same as she had before.

"Maybe nothing will happen," said Jess hopefully.

But then Evie gave a *yip*. She darted to Bella Tabbypaw, snatched her blossom drop parcel, and threw the sweets all over ground. "Look, a nice mess!" she cried.

"Oh no," said Goldie, "poor Evie already thinks she's a messy rat!"

"Hee hee!" giggled Masha. "Let's take them all!" Olivia and the Witchy Waste creatures ran into the trees, taking the rest of the stolen blossom drops with them.

"Come back!" called Mr Scruffypup. But Evie had disappeared into the forest.

Evie's mum gave a horrified cry and grasped the girls' hands in her paws. "What shall we do?"

Jess hugged her. "Don't worry," she said. "We'll get Evie back."

"We helped Olivia Nibblesqueak, remember," said Lily, putting an arm

around Hattie.

"That's right," said Goldie. "We found a spell in Mrs Taptree's library when Olivia started behaving like a bat. It stopped the messy magic before and it can do it again!"

Jess reached into her pocket and pulled out the little sketchbook she always carried with her.

"I copied it down," she said, flicking through the pages. "Listen – it's a spell to turn you back to your normal self.

You want to be yourself again?

Then here's what you must do.

Gather up those favourite things

That mean the most to you.

What do you like to do the most?

What food do you love the best?

And what is your biggest secret?

Now here's a little test.

Put them in your favourite place,

The place you love to be.

If someone names those things aloud,

Yourself once more you'll be."

Hattie Scruffypup's face brightened. "So we need to find Evie's favourite things?"

"Exactly!" Lily beamed. "If we do that, we can save her!"

CHAPTER FOUR

Ellie's Surprise

Mrs Scruffypup dabbed her eyes. "Let me see… Evie's favourite food is blossom drops," she said, her eyes filling with tears. "But those horrible Witchy Waste creatures have taken them all."

"Don't cry," Lily said. "Maybe the Nibblesqueaks will make some more."

"Of course we will!" Olivia said. "But we'll need lots more honeysuckle. It takes twenty blossoms to make one single blossom drop."

Mr Scruffypup's ears pricked up. "Follow me," he said. "I know where we can find some!"

Goldie, the girls and all the other animals followed him around Petal Hill to a tall tree. It was covered in curling stems of honeysuckle, but all the flowers on the lower branches had been picked. The rest were too high to reach, even for the girls.

"Oh no! How can we get those

flowers?" asked Jess.

"I know!" cried Lily. "Mr Cleverfeather,
can you use your Petal Puffer to blow
them off?"

"Of course!" the owl said. "Anything to
help little Evie Puffyscrup!"

He aimed the puffer upwards and
pressed the button.

Shoo-woosh!

Honeysuckle flowers blew into the air
and showered down.

All the animals hurried around
gathering the flowers, and the girls soon
had arms full of blossoms. It was like

holding a soft, scented cloud.
Hattie bounded over, clutching a
little basket. Lily and Jess filled it up
to the brim with flowers. "Olivia's
too little to carry the basket,"
Hattie said, "so I'll take it back to
the bakery for her."

She and Olivia ran off into
the trees.

"That's Evie's favourite food
sorted," said Goldie. "Now,

what's her favourite hobby?"

"Collecting things!" said Mrs
Scruffypup. "Evie's bedroom's full of her
collections. Come and see."

They went back to the Scruffypups'
den, and Mr and Mrs Scruffypup led them
upstairs to a pretty pink bedroom. The
shelves and a little desk were crammed

with pretty things. On the windowsill was
a pressed leaf collection, and beside the
bed was a pile of conkers. Hanging from
the ceiling was a collection of nuts, which
were strung together on grass stalks.

Goldie gazed around the room. "These
are wonderful," she said. "But which is
Evie's favourite?"

Mrs Scruffypup's face lit up. "That's
easy!" she exclaimed.

She crouched down, lifted the edge of
Evie's frilled quilt cover and felt around
beneath the bed. After a few moments, she
stood up again.

"That's funny," Mrs Scruffypup said.
She looked around with a puzzled
expression. "Evie's favourite is her jewel
collection. She keeps it in a little woven
basket under her bed, but it's gone.
Perhaps she left it behind the last time she
went to get more jewels?"

Mr Scruffypup gave a yap of worry. "If
we can't find Evie's favourite collection,
Goldie and the girls can't help her."

 55

"We won't give up," Lily said determinedly. "Where does Evie go to find the jewels?"

"The cavern beneath Toadstool Glade, I think," Mrs Scruffypup said.

"Of course!" said Jess. "It's got jewels on the ceiling! We saw them during our adventure with Bella Tabbypaw. Don't worry, we'll save Evie!"

Lily, Jess and Goldie hurried from Petal Hill, making their way through the forest towards Toadstool Glade.

On the way, they passed the Treasure Tree, where the forest animals got all the

food they needed.
A tiny pair of red
wellies stood at the
bottom.

"Quack, quack,
quack!" said an
unhappy voice above
them. Ellie Featherbill
the duckling swung
down on one of the
ropes that dangled
from the tree.

"Hello, Ellie!"

said Lily. "What's the matter?"

The duckling hugged the girls. "I came to get blackberries for Mum to make a pie," she explained, "but they've all gone!"

Jess held Ellie's wingtip to help her balance while she put her wellies on.

Ellie put one foot in.

Squelch!

"Yuck!' she said, and her feathers quivered. She pulled her foot out. It was covered in squished blackberry. "Yucky!" she quacked, and jumped up and down, trying to shake the mess off.

The girls peered inside Ellie's wellies.

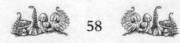

They were full of blackberries!

"That was a nasty surprise!" said Jess.

"You poor thing!"

Ellie looked upset. "Who would be horrible enough to do that?"

The girls and Goldie shared a glance.

"Evie loves surprises, doesn't she?" said Lily. "It must be her and Masha!"

CHAPTER FIVE

The Jewel Cavern

Lily gently wiped the duckling's foot with velvety moss while Jess explained what had happened to Evie.

"So Evie didn't mean to be unkind," Jess said. "She just can't help it at the moment. Masha's spell is making her love mess — and naughty surprises too!"

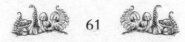

Goldie came over with her paws full of raspberries. She popped them in Ellie's basket. "There aren't any blackberries left, but these will make a nice pie," she said.

Ellie's eyes sparkled. "Thanks, Goldie!" she quacked.

The girls and Goldie hugged the duckling goodbye, then hurried through the forest.

After a while, Goldie stopped and held up a paw. "Something's moving ahead," she said. "Maybe it's Evie and Masha."

They heard a sharp giggle. "Hee hee!"

Goldie whirled around, her ears

pricked. "I can't tell where it's coming from," she said.

"Perhaps that naughty pair are following us," suggested Lily.

"Let's not worry about them for now," said Jess. "We need that jewel collection. Come on!"

They hurried on and finally emerged from the trees near the entrance to one of the tunnels leading to the cavern.

Lily jumped as a twig snapped, right above her head. She looked up.

"Evie and Masha!" she cried. "So they *were* following us!"

The little black
and white puppy
shouted, "Surprise!"
and threw a big
pawful of blackberries at Lily.

"Stop!" Jess cried, but the only reply she
got was a splatter of juicy ripe berries in
her curly blonde hair.

Evie laughed as Masha threw more
blackberries. They splattered against the
trees, covering the bark in sticky juice.

"Hee! What a lovely mess!" said Masha.
She hurried off, Evie following after her
– but instead of bounding as she usually

did, Evie scuttled with her body close to the ground.

"She's behaving just like a rat!" said Lily with a groan.

Jess nodded. "We've got to lift Masha's spell before she turns into a rat for good. Come on, let's hurry!"

They quickly cleaned off the purple blackberry mush as best they could, then went into the tunnel. It wasn't as dark as it was the last time they were there, when they went to rescue Bella Tabbypaw.

"Mr Fuzzybrush the fox dug holes in the tunnel roof so the sun can shine in and light the way," said Goldie. "Now all the animals can come and see the jewels."

"Look, Jess!" said Lily, as they approached the huge cavern. "I'd forgotten how big it was."

Jess gazed in awe at the cavern roof, which was studded with brilliantly glittering jewels of every colour.

"How does little Evie manage to

reach them?" Jess wondered.

"She doesn't need to," Goldie smiled. "Look down."

The girls gasped. Now the cavern was lighter, they saw something they'd never noticed before. The floor of the cave was dotted with beautiful jewels, too!

"Wow!" said Jess.

"There are so many!" Lily said, gazing at the glittering stones.

"We must find Evie's collection," said Jess. "Remember, she kept it in a woven basket. Let's get looking."

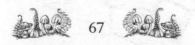

Lily searched a pile of fallen rocks, while Jess looked in all the nooks and crevices along the far wall. Goldie searched behind the great columns that supported the roof.

They'd only been looking for a few minutes when Jess heard Lily cry, "I've found it! And something else, too."

Goldie and Jess ran to see.

The little basket had fallen on its side, spilling out colourful jewels.

"Look at Evie's wonderful collection!" said Goldie. "They're all different shapes – round ones, square ones…"

"Even a heart-shaped one," said Jess, as

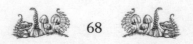

she piled the jewels back into the basket.

"Look," said Lily. She picked up some string lying close by. "Evie must have been making something."

A few paces away, they found a neat pile of golden leaves and golden twigs.

"Whatever was Evie making?" Jess wondered. "We'd better hang on to them – we might need them for our spell."

Several tunnels led out of the cavern. They couldn't decide which one to take until Lily noticed something on the floor at one of the entrances. A golden leaf. Just a little further on was another one.

"Evie must have dropped them," said
Jess. "You know what this means? We
can follow her trail! We know what her
favourite food is and her favourite hobby
– it might help us find out her secret."

Goldie set off. "Let's hurry," she called
back. "Evie was already behaving so
much like Masha, there can't be much
time left. If we don't break the spell, she'll
turn into a messy rat for good!"

CHAPTER SIX

Mud Pies

The trail of golden leaves led the friends through the tunnel. They came out near Willowtree River.

A tree with delicate trailing branches and golden leaves stood on the riverbank. "So that's where Evie got the leaves from," said Jess, pointing.

Perched up in the tree, where the trunk divided into five branches, was a tiny little cottage.

"It's so pretty," said Lily, looking closer at the willow twig walls and the plaited reed roof.

The door opened, and out popped a kingfisher! Her beak opened in surprise.

"Jess and Lily!" she said. "And Goldie, too!"

It was Mrs Blueflash! She and her family had helped the girls in their adventures before.

"Chicks!" the kingfisher called, and the

whole family flew out to flutter around the girls' heads, blowing kisses with their wingtips.

"Mrs Blueflash, we need help," said Jess. She explained about Evie and her pile of golden leaves.

"Evie has a special secret," said Lily. "We must discover what it is, otherwise

she'll turn into a rat, like Masha from the Witchy Waste. Do you know anything about it?"

"All I know is that Evie wanted some of our golden leaves for a surprise present she's making." Mrs Blueflash said.

"What is it?" Goldie asked.

"Who's it for?" asked Jess.

Mrs Blueflash shook her head. "I'm afraid I don't know."

Splat!

"Ow!" cried Lily. A big, sloppy ball of mud had hit her on the arm. "Oh, yuck. Who threw—"

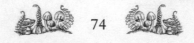

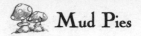

Splat!

More mud hit the Blueflashes' cottage,
and ran gloopily down the front window.

Splat!

Another splodged all over Jess's hair.
"Ugh!" she cried. "Evie and Masha must
have followed us here!"

"There they are!" said Mrs Blueflash,
pointing her wing across the river. "Chee-
kee! Chee-kee!" she cried.

Jess and Lily looked towards the
opposite bank. There, giggling away,
was Evie with Masha, Peep, Snippit
and Hopper. They were bending back a

 75

springy tree branch and loading it with mud. When they let go of the branch, the mud catapulted across the river.

Evie scurried to the water's edge. "SURPRISE!" she yelled, then turned to Masha. "We should throw mud all around the rest of the forest too!"

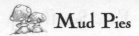

"Ooh yes," said the rat, "then it'll be lovely and messy." She launched another mud missile.

"Oh no," Mrs Blueflash squawked. "Mud is very bad for feathers! Hurry, children, hide!"

"Over here!" a small voice called to the girls.

Lily and Jess turned to see the smallest kingfisher chick hiding among the leaves of a bush. They dived behind it, Lily grabbing Goldie's paw and pulling her with them.

The chick was shaking with fright, so

Lily carefully lifted her up and stroked her feathers soothingly.

"I'm Bethany," the chick said, her voice trembling, "and Evie's my friend. I really want her back to normal!" She gave a sob.

"Don't worry," said Jess. "We'll help her. But we must find out about her secret present."

"I'm sorry," Bethany said sadly, wiping her eyes with a wing. "I don't know what it is." Her face brightened. "But I think I know where it's hidden!"

"That's brilliant!" said Lily. "Do you think you could show us?"

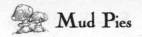

Bethany gave another tremble, but then she puffed up her feathers. "Yes," she said determinedly, "I'll show you. I'd do anything to save Evie."

"Thank you!" said Goldie, stroking the chick's bright blue and orange feathers.

"Mum, I'm going to help Evie!" Bethany called.

"Please be careful!" Mrs Blueflash called back.

"We'll look after her!" Jess promised. And they hurried away after Bethany, dodging the balls of mud that whizzed all around them.

CHAPTER SEVEN

A Secret in Petal Dell

Bethany led Goldie and the girls back towards Petal Hill. Mr and Mrs Scruffypup and Hattie were waiting anxiously outside their den.

"I've got the blossom drops from Olivia," said Hattie, holding up a full basket. Her eyes were wide with worry.

 81

"Have you found all of Evie's favourite things yet?"

"Just one more to go," said Jess. She turned to the kingfisher chick. "Bethany's helping us!"

The kingfisher fluttered over and perched on Jess's outstretched hand. "It's this way!" she chirped.

Hattie tucked the basket over her paw. "I'm coming to help," she said. "I miss Evie so much!"

Bethany zoomed up Petal Hill. Goldie and Hattie followed, bounding easily between the blossom-laden bushes.

A surprise awaited them. At the top of the hill, the ground dipped into a hidden flowery dell. It was like a little sheltered valley, and the scent of jasmine hung in the warm air. The grass was soft and cushiony and in the middle was a copse of blossom-covered pear trees. Petals fluttered down as they swayed in the breeze.

"This is Petal Dell," said Bethany.

"Over here!" Goldie called.

The girls and Hattie ran up the slope to join her. Goldie pointed at the flowers. Most of them were yellow, but in the middle, dark blue flowers were arranged into shapes.

"They're planted in the shapes of letters!" Lily cried.

Hattie gasped. "They're spelling out a word – my name! Look, they say 'Hattie'!"

Then Bethany called from the pear trees. "Come and see!" she chirped.

Goldie and the girls ran down past the flowers, into the trees. Bright balloons and streamers hung from every branch.

"It's decorated for a party!" said Jess.

Lily spotted something glinting beneath

a starflower bush, and picked it up. It was

a beautiful little crown, made of golden

willow leaves and decorated with brilliant

jewels.

"This must be what Evie was making,"

she said, showing the others.

Jess gave a cry. "Oh! Now I know what

the surprise is! Evie was planning a party for you, Hattie!"

Hattie clapped her paws together in delight.

"And this must be a crown she's made for you," Lily smiled, placing it gently on Hattie's head.

"Blossom Day is the day before my birthday," Hattie said, her eyes shining. "I always feel a bit sad because everyone's always tired after the celebrations, so my birthday doesn't feel very special. I've never told Evie, but she must have guessed!"

"And so she decided to give you a secret surprise party," said Lily.

Bethany nodded. "Evie thinks this is the prettiest place in the whole of Friendship Forest," she chirped. "That must be why she decided to have it here."

Hattie smiled. "Evie's the best little sister a puppy could have."

"And thanks to you," Jess smiled, "we've got everything we need to turn her back into her normal puppy self." She took the basket of blossom drops from Hattie and put it down. "Her favourite food!"

Lily added the basket of jewels. "Her favourite things."

"Her secret is the surprise party for Hattie," said Goldie, as Hattie lay down the crown, "and her favourite place is Petal Dell." Her ears pricked up. "Can you hear giggling?"

The girls listened. A moment later, they heard it, too.

"Evie and Masha must have followed us again," Lily whispered.

"They're probably planning another

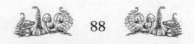

horrible, messy surprise," Jess said softly. She drew a sharp breath. "Shhhh! They're coming!"

Masha and Evie scuttled out from the bushes nearby.

"What's going on?" Masha demanded. She sat up on her back legs, chattering her teeth, and Evie did the same. Her tufty, scruffy coat was now as filthy as Masha's dirty fur. Hattie gave a cry of horror as she saw her sister.

Lily hugged Hattie. "Don't worry, we've got all Evie's favourite things. We'll save your sister!"

But Evie scooped up a big pawful of mud from the ground. *Squelch!* The mud splattered over her favourite things.

"That was fun!" giggled Evie, and she and Masha laughed loudly at the mess.

"She doesn't even recognise them," Jess said, her tummy twisting with worry. "What if we're too late?"

CHAPTER EIGHT

Party Time!

"We can't give up now," said Goldie. "Let's do the spell – and quickly!"

As Evie and Masha scooped up more mud, Jess chanted, "Evie's favourite hobby… collecting jewels!"

"Evie's favourite food," shouted Goldie. "Blossom drops!"

 91

"Evie's secret...a special surprise party!" added Lily.

They joined hands and said together, "In Evie's favourite place – Petal Dell!"

Purple sparks flew from Evie. Her tufty fur stood all on end for a moment, and then the dirt disappeared so that her white tummy was as snowy white as before.

She blinked a couple of times, then her tail began to wag.

"Hooray!" cried Lily and Jess.

"Evie's herself again," Goldie said, with tears of joy in her green eyes.

For a moment, the puppy seemed confused. She looked at Masha, then at the girls, then at Hattie. Finally, she gave a yap and bounded over to her sister. "What happened?" she asked.

Lily ruffled the white tufts above Evie's nose. "Naughty Masha put a spell on you," she explained, "but everything's fine now."

Masha's teeth chattered crossly again. "This is no good," she grumbled.

 93

"Evie's no fun anymore."

Goldie looked at Masha sternly. "It's not nice to mess up the forest," she told the rat.

"But it's so much fun!" said Masha. Her face brightened. "I'm going to go and find my other friends so we can carry on being messy!"

She scurried down Petal Hill.

Goldie sighed. "If only we could make the Witchy Waste creatures go home again," she said. "But I just can't think how."

Bethany had flown up high up to

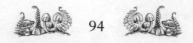

watch Masha leave. She suddenly
did an about-turn and zoomed back.
"Something's coming!" she said, and
perched on Lily's shoulder, gripping
tightly with her little feet.

A yellow-green orb appeared over the
top of the hill. Lily and Jess knew what
that meant. Grizelda!

The orb burst in a shower of stinky
sparks. There stood the witch, her green
hair writhing madly. She was so angry
that her face was almost as purple as
her tunic.

Grizelda stamped her foot. "Masha

might have failed," she screeched, "but just you wait! Soon Snippit and Hopper will cast their magic on those silly animals and Friendship Forest will be mine! Ha!"

She snapped her fingers and disappeared in a burst of smelly sparks.

"It's over," Goldie said, putting an arm around Hattie and Evie. "Let's go home."

It was early evening in Petal Dell and everyone was enjoying Hattie's birthday party. Olivia and the other Nibblesqueaks had brought lots of yummy treats from their bakery. There were cheesy twisters, fruit pies, honey biscuits, and three types of cake: raspberry cream sponge, lemon roll, and a birthday cake covered with Nibblesqueaks' Famous Nectar Icing. Olivia had iced *Happy Birthday, Hattie!* on it.

Hattie was wearing her birthday crown. "This is the best surprise ever, Evie," she said. "It's brilliant!"

"Having your party a day early was part of the surprise," Evie said happily, as Hattie pulled her into a hug. "I'm so glad you like it!"

Mr Cleverfeather had brought his Music-o-Matic. It was an enormous machine with a trumpet, drum, harp and xylophone that played themselves. Whenever anyone pressed a button and shouted, "all change!" a different tune played.

The Scruffypups were so delighted to have Evie back that they couldn't stop dancing. The Longwhiskers family got

everyone joining in the bunny hop, while the Blueflash family flew back and forth so the setting sun's rays glinted on their orange and blue feathers.

Soon it was time for Jess and Lily to go home. Evie and Hattie hugged them goodbye.

"Thank you so much for saving me," said Evie. Her fur was even scruffier than usual because she'd been dancing so much!

"You're very welcome," said Lily, giving her another cuddle.

Everyone waved goodbye.

"Snippit and Hopper will cast their spells soon, won't they?" Jess said as Goldie led the girls to the Friendship Tree.

"When they do, we'll be ready to help stop them," promised Lily.

Goldie smiled and squeezed their hands with her paws. "You're the best friends we animals could wish for."

She touched the trunk and a door opened. The girls hugged Goldie and stepped into golden shimmering light. They felt the tingle that told them they were returning to their normal size and, as the light faded, they found themselves back in Brightley Meadow. The sun was still high. No time ever passed while they were in Friendship Forest!

"That was an amazing adventure," said Lily with a smile.

"I know!" Jess grinned. "I can't wait until next time."

They made their way back to Jess's garden, kicking up heaps of red, yellow and gold autumn leaves as they went. When they looked up at the chestnut tree, the little squirrel still sat on a branch, looking down at them.

Jess offered him a nut. Both girls held

their breath as the squirrel scampered
down the tree, paused, then hopped
over to Jess. He took the nut and ran off
towards the garden shed.

"What's he doing?" asked Jess. "I
thought squirrels buried their nuts."

"He is burying
it," Lily giggled,
"in one of your
dad's wellies!"

Jess burst out
laughing. "That'll
give Dad a
surprise!"

The two girls shared a smile. They knew a little puppy who loved to give surprises!

The End

Mean witch Grizelda has used her horrid magic on poor Chloe Slipperslide the otter.

Can Lily and Jess find all Chloe's favourite things and break the spell? Find out in the next adventure,

Chloe Slipperslide's Secret

Turn over for a sneak peek . . .

"Run!" Goldie yelled to the animals. "Quick, before Snippit casts his spell on you!"

The crow was already ruffling his scruffy feathers, and purple sparks were flying about him. The animals fled in panic, rushing to hide in the trees and bushes.

But when Lily looked back, she was horrified to see that Chloe hadn't moved.

"Chloe! Run!" Lily cried.

But Chloe just crouched with her paws over her eyes and her long tail quivering.

"She's too scared to move," cried Jess.

"I'll get her!"

But before she could reach Chloe, purple sparks splattered over the frightened little otter.

Lily gasped. "Oh no! Snippit's put a spell on Chloe!"

Read

Chloe Slipperslide's Secret

to find out what happens next!

Magic
Animal Friends

Find out what happens with Peep, Masha,
Snippet and Hopper in Magic Animal
Friends series three!

COMING SOON!
Look out for
Jess and Lily's
next adventure:
Mia Floppyear's
Snowy Adventure

3 stories
in 1!

www.magicanimalfriends.com

 # Puzzle Fun!

Evie Scruffypup is throwing a surprise party for her sister, Hattie!

Can you spot the differences between these two pictures?

ANSWERS

Lily and Jess's Animal Facts

Lily and Jess love lots of different animals –
both in Friendship Forest
and in the real world.

Here are their top facts about

BORDER COLLIES

like Evie Scruffypup

- Evie Scruffypup is a breed of working dog called a border collie.

- Working dogs have been used for the last 12,000 years, mostly for herding sheep, cattle, goats and other farm animals.

- Border collies like Evie are the most intelligent dog species in the world.

- Some border collies have learned to react to hundreds of words and whistles for all different types of jobs.

- Border collies usually have litters of 6 puppies.

Tiggywinkles.
Worlds Leading Wildlife Hospital

Lily's parents aren't the only ones who run a wildlife hospital.

Have you heard of Tiggywinkles – the world's busiest wildlife hospital? They take care of over 10,000 poorly animals every year and treat all kinds of wildlife, including hedgehogs, badgers, birds, foxes and deer.

If you are worried about a wild animal, you can have a look at their website for hints and tips about what to do.

www.tiggywinkles.com

Orchard Books supports Tiggywinkles.

Registered Charity No. 286447 Tiggywinkles,
Aston Road, Haddenham, Aylesbury,
Buckinghamshire HP17 8AF UK
Tel: 01844 292292
Email: mail@sttiggywinkles.org.uk

Magic
Animal Friends
Can you keep the secret?

There's lots of fun for everyone at
www.magicanimalfriends.com

Play games and explore the secret world of
Friendship Forest, where animals can talk!

Join the
Magic Animal Friends Club!

Special competitions

Exclusive content

All the latest Magic Animal Friends news!

To join the Club, simply go to

www.magicanimalfriends.com/join-our-club/